JOHNNY CAT
THE CAT IN BLACK

Written by Timothy James Rozon

Tellwell Talent
www.tellwell.ca

ISBN
978-0-2288-8266-4 (Hardcover)
978-0-2288-8267-1 (Paperback)
978-0-2288-8265-7 (eBook)

For Dylan River

People always look for the pot of gold at the end of the rainbow, but they forget they're looking at a rainbow.

There is a legend of a cat all dressed in black and their name is Johnny Cat.

There is a guitar-playing cat who was born with an old soul.

There is a cool cat who is always in control.

There is a cat all dressed in black who loves to rock and roll!

There is a cat who loves to sing.

There is a cat who likes to swing.

There is a cat all dressed in black because it's just their thing.

There is a cat that loves to play and who dreams all day.

There is a cat who's kind and bright.

There is a cat who shines in the light.

There is a cat who won't wear red or blue.

They won't wear green or yellow.

They won't wear orange or purple.

*Not the shiniest of silver, not even gold.

The only colour cool enough to be worn by Johnny Cat is Black, I'm told.

Johnny in black, is the happiest Cat!

Meow.

Timothy Rozon is a Canadian actor,
author and father.

Ingram Content Group UK Ltd.
Milton Keynes UK
UKRC030113190423
420242UK00003BA/4

9 780228 882664